TROUBLE at TABLE 5

#1:
The Candy Caper

Check out all the

TROUBLE at TABLE 5

books!

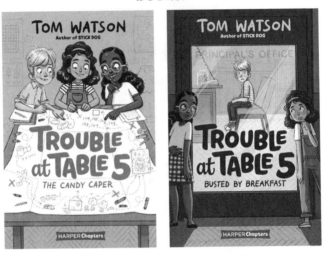

#1   #2

Read more books by **Tom Watson**

#1-12   #1-5

TROUBLE at TABLE 5

#1:
The Candy Caper

by **Tom Watson**

illustrated by
Marta Kissi

HARPER Chapters

An Imprint of HarperCollinsPublishers

Dedicated to Mary
(TFSMFTG)

Trouble at Table 5 #1: The Candy Caper
Text copyright © 2020 by Tom Watson
Illustrations copyright © 2020 by HarperCollins Publishers
Illustrations by Marta Kissi
www.harperchapters.com
Library of Congress Control Number: 2019950101
ISBN 978-0-06-295341-4 — ISBN 978-0-06-295340-7 (pbk.)
Typography by Torberg Davern
20 21 22 23 24   PC/LSCC   10 9 8 7 6 5 4 3 2 1
❖
First Edition

Table of Contents

CHAPTER ONE
THINGS GET STUCK IN MY HEAD

I'M MOLLY.

I get things stuck in my head sometimes. I'll give you a few examples.

This morning, I had Froot Loops for breakfast. Froot Loops come in six different colors—red, orange, yellow, green, purple, and blue. When I poured the dry cereal into my bowl, I took the purple and green ones out. That's because purple and green remind me of grapes.

And I don't like grapes because they come in big bunches and it's hard to tell how many are in a bunch. I like to know how many things there are. That's just me.

So, I only had red, blue, orange, and yellow Froot Loops in my bowl. I ate all the blue ones first. It's kind of hard to get only blue Froot Loops on your spoon, but it's worth it. When I only had red, orange, and yellow Froot Loops left, I just ate them all. They could be mixed up. That's because red and yellow make orange, so those Froot Loops are allowed to be together.

See what I mean?

Oh, I also couldn't be done until I knew all the Froot Loops were gone.

I needed to know that there wasn't one hiding beneath the milk at the bottom of the bowl. I sort of splashed my spoon in the milk to make sure there wasn't one left.

My dad asked, "Molly, what are you doing?"

"I'm making sure there aren't any more Froot Loops in my bowl," I answered. "It's important."

This made perfectly good sense to my dad. Both my parents understand me very well.

So do Rosie and Simon. They are my two best friends.

Here are a few more quick examples.

The socks in my sock drawer are folded flat. They're not rolled up in balls. Flat things are not supposed to be rolled up.

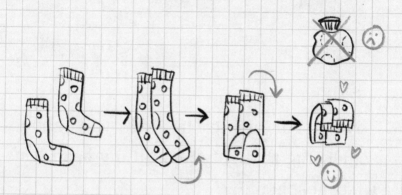

Also, if I start a book, I can't read anything else until I finish that book. I can't read a different book. Or a magazine. Or a comic book. I have to finish that book first.

And my pillows need to be in a certain order before I get into bed. They need to be like this:

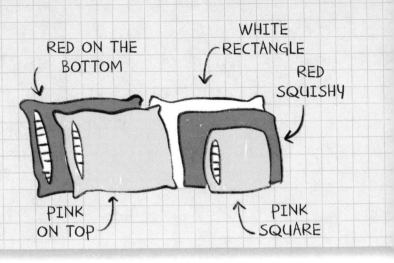

RED ON THE BOTTOM

WHITE RECTANGLE

RED SQUISHY

PINK ON TOP

PINK SQUARE

It's just who I am.

Now I'm going to tell you about something that got stuck in my head last week at school.

Mr. Willow asked me to take the absentee slip to the main office. It's the piece of paper he fills out after taking attendance in the morning. I went to the office and turned the slip in to Mrs. Beyersdoerfer. We just call her Mrs. B.

"Here's the absentee slip, Mrs. B.," I said and handed it to her.

"Thanks, Molly," she said and took it from me. She put it on top of the stack of absentee slips from the other classes.

"You're welcome," I answered.

Butrightwhen I turnedtoleave, something caught my eye.

Something in Principal Shelton's office. Her office is off to the side of the main office. It has a door with a window.

There was something colorful in her office.

On her desk.

In a big glass jar.

And it got stuck in my head.

ONE CHAPTER
DOWN. OFF TO A
GREAT START!

CHAPTER TWO

UH-OH

I HUSTLED BACK to Mr. Willow's class and sat down at our table. I share Table 5, in the back, with Simon and Rosie.

"Uh-oh," Rosie said. Rosie is a nickname for Rosa.

"What?" I asked.

She didn't answer. Instead, she poked Simon with her elbow and nodded her head in my direction.

Simon looked at me. Simon isn't a nickname for anything. It's just Simon. He said, "Oh no."

They nodded at each other and then looked at me some more.

"What?" I asked again.

Rosie said, "There's something going on with you."

"No, there's not."

"Yes, there is," Simon said. "What is it?"

"Nothing," I answered—even though I knew there really was something.

"You're having one of your moments," Rosie said. "We can see it in your eyes."

"No, I'm not."

"Yes, you are, Molly," Simon said. "We've seen this look, like, a million times. It's the exact same look you got before we jumped into the leaf pile a few weeks ago.

I mean, every single leaf? Seriously?"

Rosie pleaded, "Just tell us."

"Okay," I said. I knew they were right. This thing was not going to get out of my head. "There's a mason jar on Principal Shelton's desk. It's the kind of jar my mom uses to make raspberry jam. She gives the jam out at Christmas."

"What's so special about the jar on Principal Shelton's desk?" asked Simon.

I answered, "It's full of Skittles."

"And?" Rosie asked.

"I want to know how many Skittles are in that jar," I whispered. I had to be quiet because Mr. Willow doesn't like talking. I'd seen Simon get in trouble enough to know that. He can be a total chatterbox sometimes. Mr. Willow has even called Simon's parents before. And I definitely didn't want that to happen to me. "I *need* to know how many Skittles are in that jar."

"We can't sneak into the principal's office, dump out a bunch of Skittles, count them, and then put them back without anyone noticing," Rosie said. "We'll totally get caught."

"And totally suspended," Simon added.

"I need to know," I said.

"It's one thing to not jump into the leaves until every single leaf in the yard is in the pile, Molly," Rosie said, shaking her head. "And then if another leaf falls, we have to stop jumping, go get that leaf, and add it to the pile. But this is different."

Simon agreed, "Way different."

All I said was, "I need to know."

"This could mean, like, getting into

serious trouble at school," Rosie said, still shaking her head.

"And at home," added Simon.

"I need to know."

Rosie looked at Simon. Simon looked at Rosie. Then they both looked at me. We were good friends. Best friends even. They knew me. They knew nothing would change my mind.

"You need to know," Simon said.

"I need to know."

"Okay," Rosie said. She twirled her hair around her left index finger. I knew this was a good sign. "We're going to need a plan."

But we couldn't come up with a Skittles-snatching-and-counting strategy right then. That's because Mr. Willow was already walking toward us.

"Table 5," he said in a voice a little louder than usual. "Quiet down. Everybody get your composition books out."

"Lunchtime," I whispered.

"Lunchtime," Rosie and Simon whispered back in unison.

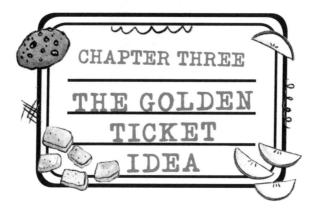

CHAPTER THREE

THE GOLDEN TICKET IDEA

ROSIE, SIMON, AND I sat at the table farthest away from the food—and farthest away from everybody else. Lunch was grilled cheese, tater tots, apple slices, and a chocolate chip cookie.

I counted my tater tots. There were eleven. So I gave Simon three. I like to eat warm things in even numbers—and never double digits.

So, for tater tots, I could eat two, four, six, or eight. And I was hungry, so I chose eight.

I eat even numbers for cold things too. But double digits doesn't matter for cold things. I had seven apple slices and I gave one to Rosie.

I had been putting some of my food on Rosie's and Simon's trays for a couple of years now, so they barely even noticed.

"Anybody come up with a plan to count

the Skittles?" I asked in a low voice. It wasn't quite a whisper. There wasn't anyone around us.

"Not yet," Rosie answered.

"I thought of something," Simon said. "It's kind of a bad idea though, I think."

"There are no bad ideas," Rosie said.

"Okay, here goes," Simon said after that encouragement.

When Simon talks about something he's excited about, it can be kind of strange.

He tilts his head a bit to the left and gets this glazed look in his eyes. Once he gets going, he talks faster and faster—and it's hard for him to stop.

"We need to get Principal Shelton out of her office," Simon began after tilting his head and getting that look in his eyes. "And I was thinking there must be a reason why she has all those Skittles on her desk. She must *love* Skittles. I mean, she doesn't have Tootsie Rolls or Nerds or Sour Patch Kids on her desk, right?"

"Right," Rosie said slowly. She sounded a little suspicious.

"She loves Skittles," Simon repeated. "So, we go to the store after school and buy a pack of Skittles. Then we tear it open real careful like.

1. GO TO THE STORE

2. BUY A PACK OF SKITTLES

3. OPEN

4. DESIGN + PRINT THE GOLDEN TICKET

5. SLIP THE GOLDEN TICKET INSIDE

6. GLUE TO CLOSE AGAIN

DONE!

21

When we get the pack open, we slip in a golden ticket. You know, like in *Charlie and the Chocolate Factory*. We can design it on my mom's computer and print it out. We have a color printer. After we insert the ticket, we glue the Skittles packet back up and then put it on her desk the next day."

"What's the ticket say?" I asked.

Simon told us proudly.

CONGRATULATIONS!
YOU'VE WON A FREE TRIP TO THE
SKITTLES FACTORY
IN MIAMI, FLORIDA!
MUST LEAVE NOW!

"Then when she leaves, the hard part's done," he said. "With her office empty, Molly just needs to sneak in. You know, through the window or the heating vents or whatever. Dump out the Skittles and start counting. Easy stuff."

THE JAR

"Umm, Simon," Rosie said slowly. "You know how I said there are no bad ideas?"

"Yeah," he answered as he untilted his head.

Rosie giggled. "That's sort of a bad idea."

"Yeah," Simon said. His feelings weren't hurt or anything. "I know. I just thought I'd throw it out there. Get the conversation started. I don't think she'd ever fall for it."

"But you're right about a lot of stuff," I said. I didn't want Simon to feel discouraged. "I need to get into her office—and get her out of it."

Then the bell rang.

"Does one of you want my chocolate chip cookie?" I asked.

"Don't you want it?" Rosie replied.

"No," I said and shook my head. "It's impossible to tell how many chocolate chips are inside."

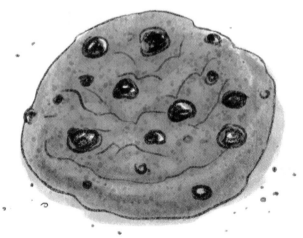

"Oh, right," Rosie said. "I forgot. I'll take it if Simon doesn't want it."

Simon said he was full.

"We can talk about the plan after school," I said as I put my cookie on Rosie's tray. Then I reached across the table and grabbed Rosie's left hand and Simon's right hand. "We *have* to come up with something. I *have* to get those Skittles out of my head."

SIMON, ROSIE, AND I either ride bikes or walk to school together. This was a walk day. So it was the perfect time to work on our plan.

"Where were we?" Rosie asked.

"We were trying to come up with a way to get me into Principal Shelton's office," I said. "That's step one. Step two is to get Shelton out of the office when I'm in there. And step three is to count the Skittles."

"Okay, let's tackle step one," Rosie said. "We need to think about this logically. Why do students go to the principal's office?"

"It's usually when somebody gets in trouble," I answered.

"That's it then," Simon said. "You just need to get into trouble."

"I don't know how," I said as we passed the mailbox on the corner.

"I've never been in trouble before. I get good grades, I don't skip class, I always help with decorations for the school play. What should I do?"

Simon had lots of ideas.

"You could let all the class pets loose," he said quickly. "There would be turtles and hamsters and bunnies everywhere. Or you can start a food fight. You know, throw a handful of french fries across the cafeteria and squirt some ketchup at somebody's head."

"Umm—" I said, trying to interrupt. But Simon was on a roll.

"Or you could go into the bathroom, unroll the toilet paper, and wrap it around the outside of the school," he went on, walking backward in front of me and Rosie as he talked.

"Or you could crumple up hundreds of pieces of paper and fill up a bunch of lockers with them. Then when people open their lockers, there's this big cascade of paper pouring out at them. Or you could turn the sink on in Mrs. Bruton's science room, plug the drain, and flood the school. Or you could—"

"Simon?" Rosie interrupted.

"Yeah?"

"How do you come up with your ideas?"

"I'm just really clever, I guess."

"Okay, umm, those are all great suggestions," I said. There was something Simon said that had sparked an idea in me. It was right at the edge of my mind— and I knew if I concentrated I could figure it out.

"Listen, you gave me an idea, I think. I'll use the toilet paper. Not quite the way you suggested. But I'll use it to get into trouble. So, I'll take care of step one— getting into the principal's office."

"Now, we need to take care of step two," Rosie said.

She stopped on the sidewalk at the end of my driveway. "Once Molly is *in*, we have to get Principal Shelton *out* of the office."

She twirled some of her hair around her left index finger. She does that when she's thinking. Rosie is super smart. Simon and I knew not to interrupt her. It took her about thirty seconds to come up with a solution.

"Okay, Molly will be inside," Rosie said,

lifting her head to look at Simon and me. "Simon, it's our job to get Principal Shelton out of her office."

"How?" asked Simon.

But instead of answering Simon's question, she asked him something instead. She said, "Do you have any flip-flops?"

"Why would I need flip-flops?"

Rosie pointed toward my house and said, "I'll tell you inside."

YOU'VE READ FOUR CHAPTERS. THAT'S 2,382 WORDS!

CHAPTER FIVE

IT'S NOT WEIRD—IT'S AWESOME!

ROSIE SAT AT the kitchen table with Simon. She could see the confusion on our faces. We had no idea what her plan was.

"Don't worry about it," Rosie said. "I've got it. Simon and I will take care of step two—getting Principal Shelton out of her office. And, Molly, you're sure you can take care of step one—getting into trouble?"

"I'm sure," I said as I put three pieces

of bread into the toaster. "I'm going to use toilet paper. You'll see."

"Are you okay with getting into trouble?" Simon asked.

"No, I'm definitely *not* okay with getting into trouble," I explained and shook my head. "But what choice do I have? I need to know how many Skittles are in that jar. That's way more important."

"Okay. Then that only leaves step three— counting those Skittles," Rosie said.

She scrunched her mouth to one side a little bit. She was sort of talking to herself as much as to us. And she was twirling her hair again. "How can we do that?"

"That part should be easy," Simon said. "With Principal Shelton gone, Molly just dumps out the jar and starts counting, right?"

"No," Rosie said and shook her head. "Step two gets Shelton out of her office. But I don't know how *long* she'll be gone.

Plus, there could be people hanging around outside the office. Mrs. B. or somebody else."

"Right," Simon agreed. "Molly needs to find a way to count the Skittles really fast."

"I don't think I can," I said, picturing that jar on Principal Shelton's desk. I got a jar of Mom's homemade raspberry jam from the refrigerator. "There must be hundreds in that jar."

Rosie snapped her fingers. She can snap extra loud.

"We could get a separate container—something smaller," Rosie said, explaining her idea. She's good at math—like, really good. "We could get a Styrofoam cup or something. We go buy some Skittles and see how many fit into the cup."

"How would that work?" I asked. I gave Simon and Rosie each a piece of toast and set the raspberry jam on the table.

"Well, let's say 127 fit into the cup," Rosie said. Using her empty hands, she pretended to pour Skittles from the jar into the Styrofoam cup. "Then when you're alone in Shelton's office you can just see how many times it takes to fill the cup. Like, maybe you can fill the cup three times and then there's 14 left over.

HOW MANY SKITTLES?

1.   = 127

2.

3.   127   127   127

4. $127 \times 3 = 381 + 14 = \boxed{395}$

39

That would be 127 times 3, which is 381. Plus 14 would be 395. That would be way faster than counting 395 Skittles individually."

"How do you do math so fast?" asked Simon, spreading jam on his toast.

"I don't know," Rosie answered modestly. "I'm weird, I guess."

Simon said, "It's not weird, it's awesome!"

Something about Rosie's idea didn't work for me. And I guess she could tell.

Rosie asked, "What is it?"

"It just doesn't sound very precise," I said. I wiped some raspberry jam from the corner of my mouth. Mom's raspberry jam is really good, but it's sticky. "I mean, it won't be the same number of Skittles in the cup every time. Sometimes it will be 127. But other times it might be 129 or 118. There's no way to be exact."

Simon said, "But you would know there are pretty close to 395 Skittles in the jar."

"You don't want to be 'pretty close,' right?" Rosie asked.

"Right," I confirmed. "I have to know the exact number. Otherwise, what's the point?"

Rosie and Simon are such good friends. They didn't question why I had to be exact. They knew it was important to me. It was just as important as eating my food in even numbers or only jumping in the leaf pile after every single leaf was raked up.

They understood.

"Okay, Molly has to get an exact count. But she also has to be fast," Simon summarized. "How in the world can she do that?"

"We *do* need to be exact," Rosie said and paused. She held her half-eaten toast midair in her right hand. She twirled some hair with her left hand. "But we *don't* have to be fast."

"What do you mean?" I asked.

"I know how to do it," Rosie said.

Simon asked, "How?"

Rosie explained how she figured out step three—how to count the Skittles.

And I thought it might just work.

We only needed to do two more things before launching our mission the next day at school.

For the first thing, I went to the sink and turned on the hot water. Rosie brought me the jar of raspberry jam.

Simon ran to the store to do the second thing.

CHAPTER SIX

IT'S TIME FOR TOILET PAPER

WE SKIPPED LUNCH the next day. I think we were all too nervous to eat anyway. It was time to launch our plan. I couldn't wait to find out how many Skittles were in Principal Shelton's jar. I thought about that a lot the previous night. It kept me up for a while.

As everybody else in third grade went to get their lunch, I met Rosie right outside the girls' bathroom.

The boys' bathroom was across the hall from the girls' bathroom. That worked out perfectly for our plan. Simon got there less than a minute after Rosie and I met.

He asked, "Did you fill it up?"

I shook my backpack so he could hear that we did.

He nodded and said, "Great."

"Do you have your flip-flops?" Rosie asked him.

Like me, he shook his backpack a little. "They're in here."

"Here are your supplies," Rosie said to him and reached into her pocket. She pulled out a small plastic baggie with a tube of superglue, a thumbtack, and some nail clippers inside. "You know what to do."

I said, "We'll meet back here in a few minutes."

Simon tiptoed into the boys' bathroom. He didn't have to tiptoe or anything. He just did it for fun and to be dramatic.

Rosie and I went into the girls' bathroom. And we got started.

Rosie pulled out the toilet paper from the giant roll in the first bathroom stall. It ran all the way from the dispenser, under the stall door and, ultimately, to Rosie's hand.

I stood in front of the sinks. I spread my legs apart and stretched my arms out wide.

Rosie wrapped that toilet paper all

around me, starting at my ankles and working her way up each leg. When she got to my stomach, Rosie held the toilet paper in one place as I turned slowly around a bunch of times. That worked much faster.

"Halfway there," Rosie whispered, biting her lip. I think she was afraid the toilet paper might tear. She definitely didn't want to start over. We didn't have a whole lot of time. Lunch period would be finished in ten minutes.

When Rosie got up to my armpits, I stopped spinning and she took over again. She wrapped my left arm and then my right arm. Finally, she wrapped my head, leaving plenty of room for my eyes, nose, and mouth.

When she was done, Rosie tore off the toilet paper and tucked that loose end underneath one of the layers at my back.

"Oh my—" Rosie said and slapped her hand over her mouth. I could see her smiling behind her hand.

"What?!"

She shook her head and put her hands on my shoulders. She turned me around to look in the mirror above the sink.

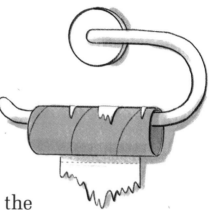

When I saw myself, I knew one thing for sure.

I was just a few minutes away from those Skittles.

HOW DO YOU THINK THIS PLAN WILL WORK OUT?

CHAPTER SEVEN

LET'S DO THIS THING

I WAS A mummy.

"You're not a very scary-looking mummy," Rosie said and panted. She needed to catch her breath a bit from laughing.

"There aren't very many mummies who are four feet, two and a half inches tall," I added, catching my breath too.

"It will have to do," Rosie said, giving her head a definitive nod. "Besides, we're not doing this to make you look scary. We're doing it so you get into trouble."

"Right," I said.

"You stay in here while I see if Simon is ready," Rosie said and began to push the bathroom door open. "You can't be standing out in the hallway like that. Once you step out this door, it's mummy time."

I nodded my mummy head.

Rosie went out in the hallway. I could hear her talking to Simon.

"You're ready?" she asked.

"Ready."

"Did the nail clippers work?"

"Totally," Simon said. I couldn't see him, but I figured he was lifting a foot up to show Rosie the bottom of his flip-flop. "They cut the head off that thumbtack perfectly. I put a little dab of superglue on it and stuck it to the bottom of my flip-flop. Easy stuff. I got some superglue between my fingers, but that was the only problem."

"Awesome," Rosie said. "I'll get Molly."

Rosie stepped back into the girls' bathroom. The second she saw me, she slapped her hand over her mouth to stifle another laugh.

"Don't laugh!"

"I can't help it," she said, taking three seconds to get control of herself. "Simon's ready. Are you ready?"

I nodded my mummy head again.

"All right then," Rosie said and leaned down to pick up my backpack. She was real careful putting my arms through the straps and positioning it on my back. She didn't want to tear the toilet paper.

"Feel okay?" she asked.

"Yeah."

Rosie said, "Let's do this thing."

And then we did that thing.

CHAPTER EIGHT
ARR-GRR-GRR-ARJ!

WHEN I STEPPED out of the bathroom, Simon made the funniest sound I ever heard. It was like he laughed, snorted, and coughed at the same time. His whole body shook, trembled, and convulsed. He didn't just hold in a laugh. He held in the biggest laugh he had ever wanted to laugh in his entire life.

"Shh!" Rosie said and giggled. "Shh!"

"I'm trying," Simon said and squeezed his arms around his belly like he was hugging himself super hard. "I'm really trying."

Rosie said, "You better get moving, Molly. Before Simon passes out."

I raised my arms in front of me mummy-style and started down the hallway. I needed to pass the third grade classrooms and the second grade classrooms before I would walk past the principal's office.

"Make some growling noises or something," Rosie said as I took my first few steps. "We'll be a few minutes behind you."

I started growling.

Arr-grr-grr-arj! Arr-grr-grr-arj!

I walked past a couple of third grade classrooms.

I started to pass the second grade classrooms.

Arr-grr-grr-arj!

But that's as far as I made it.

I heard a door open behind me.

It was Mrs. Brooks, a third grade teacher.

"What in the world?!" she said. I heard her heavy footsteps approach me from behind.

She took hold of my left elbow when she reached me.

Arr-grr-grr-arj!

"You can stop growling now," Mrs. Brooks said, shaking her head.

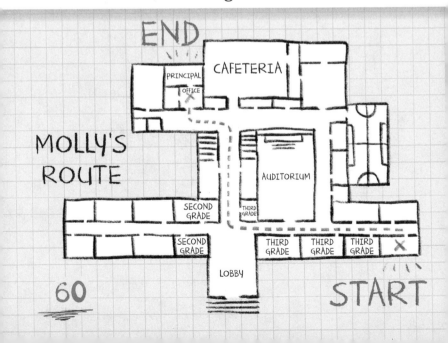

END

PRINCIPAL
OFFICE

CAFETERIA

MOLLY'S ROUTE

AUDITORIUM

SECOND GRADE

THIRD GRADE

SECOND GRADE

THIRD GRADE

THIRD GRADE

THIRD GRADE

LOBBY

START

I stopped growling. And when I did, Mrs. Brooks said the exact thing I wanted to hear.

"You're coming with me to the office. We'll see what Principal Shelton has to say about this."

I was one step—actually, several mummy steps—closer to counting those Skittles.

It has to work, I thought to myself. It *has* to work.

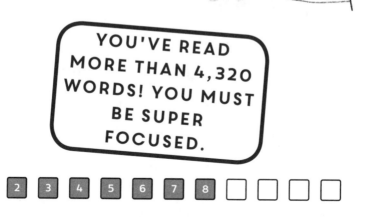

YOU'VE READ MORE THAN 4,320 WORDS! YOU MUST BE SUPER FOCUSED.

CHAPTER NINE

INSIDE THE PRINCIPAL'S OFFICE

PRINCIPAL SHELTON STOOD before me, leaning back against the front of her desk. I sat awkwardly in a chair. Some of the toilet paper had torn as I sat down.

She didn't look real mad, to be honest. She wasn't happy, that was for sure. She looked kind of angry and amused all mixed up together.

She stared down, examining me from

my mummy feet to my mummy head. I think she was trying to figure out who I was. Whenever I got the chance, I peeked around the side of her and eyeballed that big jar of Skittles. It was right where I saw it the first time.

I couldn't wait to count those things.

"You know, you're not a very frightening mummy," Principal Shelton said.

"I know," I answered.

"And I don't think mummies typically wear backpacks."

I nodded my mummy head again.

She walked behind her desk, retrieved a trash can, and placed it next to my chair. As she did, I heard the main office door open and close. I heard Rosie cough a little. I think she was trying to signal me. Rosie wanted me to know that she and Simon were there.

"All right," Principal Shelton said. "Let's find out who you are, Mummy."

I started to tear at the toilet paper around my head first.

"Molly!" Principal Shelton cried. She was obviously surprised. "Molly Dyson?!"

I nodded my non-mummy head at her.

I took my backpack off and put it on the floor. I needed it to be easy to reach when the time came.

And the time was coming soon.

I could hear Simon and Rosie talking with Mrs. B. They seemed to be stalling for time. They asked Mrs. B. about her dog, Bingo. Bingo is a beagle and Mrs. B. really likes to talk about him.

She has pictures of Bingo taped up all around her computer screen.

I tore off the toilet paper from around my arms and stomach, dumping the shreds into the trash can. Principal Shelton just stood there above me. She didn't say anything.

I was just getting to the toilet paper on my legs when I heard Rosie ask Mrs. B. if she could borrow some masking tape.

"Owww!" Simon screamed from the main office. "Oh, man! That hurts so much!"

Principal Shelton snapped her head toward the door.

Simon had initiated step two—getting Principal Shelton out of her office.

"Keep working on it, Molly," she said. "I'll be back in a minute."

CHAPTER TEN

IT HURTS SO MUCH!

"WHAT IS GOING on out here?" Principal Shelton called as she went out to the main office.

"I stepped on a tack!" Simon exclaimed. "It hurts so much!"

I leaned back in the chair and looked out the doorway. Mrs. B. and Rosie knelt in front of Simon as he held his foot up for them to see. I could see the thumbtack top on the bottom of his flip-flop.

It sure looked like there was a thumbtack stuck all the way in.

But I knew that wasn't true.

I knew the top of it was just glued there. Simon had clipped off the pointy part with the nail clippers back in the boys' bathroom.

"Aaa-oooh!" Simon groaned some more in pain—and Principal Shelton leaned down to look at his foot too.

Now was my chance.

I didn't have much time.

I unzipped my backpack and pulled out the mason jar full of Skittles.

Rosie and I had emptied the jar the day before when we were done with our after-school snack of raspberry jam on toast. We got the rest of the jam out by running hot water into the jar. While we did that, Simon ran to the grocery store and bought a bunch of Skittles.

He dropped them off at my house before going to soccer practice. Rosie and I filled the jar up almost to the top—just like the jar in Principal Shelton's office. Then we put it in my backpack.

I looked out to the main office. Rosie, Mrs. B., and Principal Shelton were huddled around Simon.

He groaned again and yelled, "No, don't touch it!"

I traded our jar for the jar on Principal Shelton's desk. I put her jar into my backpack and zipped it shut. Then I started unwrapping the toilet paper from my calves and ankles.

"Okay, okay," I heard Principal Shelton say. "We won't touch it. Go see the school nurse. Rosie, you go with him."

I leaned back and peeked out the door.

I saw Rosie help Simon up from his chair. He sort of walked-hopped-limped out of the office.

He's a pretty good actor.

Principal Shelton came back to the office.

"What is this? Bizarro day?" she muttered to herself as she returned. "I've got mummies walking the hallway.

Students stepping on sharp objects. What's next?"

She sat down at her desk and looked across it at me.

"It's time to call your parents, Molly."

That was okay with me.

I had Principal Shelton's jar of Skittles in my backpack.

Now, all I had to do was count them.

ONLY TWO MORE CHAPTERS TO GO! HOW ARE YOU FEELING?

CHAPTER ELEVEN

IT'S COUNTING TIME

ROSIE, SIMON, AND I stopped at Picasso Park on the walk home from school. We chose a picnic table to count the Skittles in Principal Shelton's jar.

I was so happy.

I was finally going to get those Skittles out of my head.

Rosie and Simon started counting.

"Stop," I said.

Simon and Rosie stopped.

"Can you guys do me a favor?"

They both nodded.

"Can we count them one color at a time?" I asked.

They smiled at me and we began to separate the Skittles into five piles—orange, yellow, green, purple, and red.

When we had them in separate color piles, Rosie asked, "Do we need to count the colors in a certain order?"

"No," I said. "But that's really, really nice of you to ask."

We counted.

And counted.

And counted.

I smiled at my two best friends. We finally knew how many Skittles were in Principal Shelton's jar.

We filled the jar back up.

Then Simon asked, "What do you want to do now?"

"I think I have to go home and get in

trouble now," I whispered. I was so, so, so happy to have the Skittles out of my head. But I really didn't want to face my parents.

"Oh, right," Rosie said.

Simon asked, "What do you think they're going to do?"

"I don't know," I answered. "I've never gotten into trouble at school before."

Rosie and Simon came one step closer to me.

"Do you want us to come with you?" Rosie asked.

"We can," Simon added.

"No," I said and shook my head. "Thanks though."

And then I grabbed my backpack and went home.

CHAPTER TWELVE
THEY'RE OUT OF MY HEAD

MOM AND DAD were waiting for me when I got home.

Do you remember when I told you that my parents understand how something can get stuck in my head and then I can't get it out? They get it. They know me. But getting in trouble with the principal was different. I didn't know what would happen.

They had already talked to Principal Shelton.

But they wanted to know what happened from me. So I explained to them how the Skittles got stuck in my head. And I told them how I *had* to find out how many Skittles were in Principal Shelton's jar. I explained why I had to get into trouble.

I told them how Simon pretended to have a thumbtack stuck in his foot.

I detailed how I switched the jars.

"You replaced the jar?" Dad asked. "And that replacement jar was full of Skittles too?"

I nodded and told them there were exactly—exactly—473 Skittles in Principal Shelton's jar.

"It's okay," Mom said when I was done explaining. "That's just who you are. You needed to know. But next time, try not to get into trouble at school. Okay?"

"Okay."

Dad asked, "What happened to the Skittles?"

"Umm," I said. It took me a few seconds to remember. I hadn't thought about those Skittles since we finished counting them. Then I remembered. "They're in my backpack."

"Well, you better bring them to me," Dad said.

"Why?" I asked and held perfectly still. I definitely didn't know why Dad wanted them.

He looked me right in the eyes and said,

"I love Skittles, that's why."

I smiled and went to get the Skittles.

We each got a handful.

I picked out the green and purple Skittles from my portion. They reminded me of grapes. So, obviously, I didn't want to eat them.

Mom and Dad ate them for me.

CONGRATULATIONS!

You've read **12** chapters,

85 pages,

and **5,777** words!

Fun and Games!

THINK

In this book, Molly, Simon, and Rosie come up with a plan to count the Skittles in the jar on the principal's desk. You can see a map of Molly's route on page 60. Draw a map of *your* school. What route would you take to the principal's office? What obstacles would you face?

FEEL

Molly just *has* to know how many Skittles are in that jar. Think of a time when you got an idea or problem stuck in your head. What did you do to unstick yourself? Did anyone help you? How did you feel when you figured it all out? Draw your facial expression when the idea was bugging you—and what you looked like when you solved the problem.

ACT

In this story, Rosie wraps Molly up in toilet paper to make her look like a mummy. What other fun, creative things can you do with toilet paper? Here's one idea: Draw a target on a piece of cardboard, with the highest score in the middle. Then take a wad of toilet paper, get it wet, squeeze out the extra water, and throw it at the target. It will stick! Keep score and everything.

Don't miss the next **TROUBLE at TABLE 5** **book!**

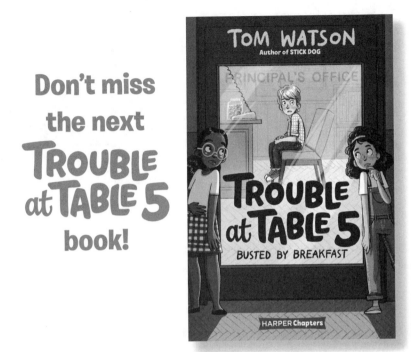

Mission: Get OUT of trouble!

When Simon gets in trouble for talking too much in class, his friends at Table 5 have his back. They need to think up a plan to keep Simon from getting grounded—*and fast*! With help from Molly and Rosie, Simon just might have a chance.

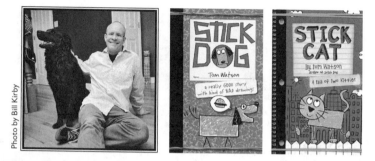

Tom Watson is the author of the popular STICK DOG and STICK CAT series. And now he's the author of this new series, TROUBLE AT TABLE 5. Tom lives in Chicago with his wife and kids and their big dog, Shadow. When he's not at home, Tom's usually out visiting classrooms all over the country. He's met a lot of students who remind him of Molly, Simon, and Rosie. He's learned that kids are smarter than adults. Like, way smarter.

Marta Kissi is originally from Warsaw but now lives in London where she loves bringing stories to life. She shares her art studio with her husband, James, and their pet plant, Trevor.